MW01172575

LOVE IN THE
WEIRDEST PLACES

Michael Spencer Sr

CONTENT

1

HEAVY LIFT

Sometimes, life gets so hard and difficult. We have days that seem too unbearable to get through. The weight of the world comes down on us, and it seems like it will not end. Often, we feel even while in a relationship that we are all alone.

We go through relationships that seem to drag us down and make life even worse. We think because we are in a relationship that things will always be great, but that is far from the truth. It can be a hit and miss, so we must take it as it comes.

We need that person who is a forklift in our life. When I was in the military, I loved driving the forklift. It was so easy to use and made my job much easier. It could lift everything that I could not. So, I relied on the forklift to be a part of my daily use. I did what I could, but when things got heavy, I always knew I could count on my personal forklift to help lift the burden to accomplish a task, get through the day or even gave me the motivation to assist someone else who also had a heavy burden.

When you get that one person in your life who knows you will struggle, have bad days, occasionally be moody, or have down days, but will never leave your side no matter what, that is the person that you need in your life. It does not give you permission to be difficult to deal with, but it allows you to know that when you are not at your best, you can rest assure that they will not abandon you and will always be there to give you that uplift that you desperately need.

2

ENGINE BAY DOOR

All aircraft have one major thing in common, regardless of the model type. They all have an engine bay door. What makes this so unique is that when you open it up, you have access to so much. Of course, we all know that each aircraft's most important part is the engine. No engine, no flying.

While all that is important, the engine bay door is special because it is like the heart of all planes. Each door varies in the number of hinges that are required to be undone to open the door, but once it is open, you see everything. This is the only time that repairs of any issues can be performed.

When opened up hoses are crossed over each other, oil, electrical tape on wires, and so on. To the average eye, they will see this but will have no idea how to adjust and comprehend what they are seeing. The one thing that is sure and certain, once the door is open, everything is available to be seen. No more hiding anything!

Being in a relationship, we all want to get to that point where we will not be judged by what is seen when we open our engine door but embraced and loved. When we do that, we can start to be repaired from the inside out. After all, it is what is not seen that needs the most repairing.

When you are in a relationship, and your partner decides to open their door, be there for support. Help them through the process of healing. When they are closed up on the inside, it is hard to love others the way it was meant to be. Don't be afraid to let your door open, so those around you can help you heal.

We all have our different hoses crossed up, but together with the right person, the repair cycle can begin. We must be willing to let someone open us so we can be the person they desire us to be, and the love of their life. If the hinges are never undone and the door is never swung open, repairs and healing will never take place.

3

SPEED WILL RUIN IT

Some things in life are just meant to be slow. No matter how fast you want it to go, it cannot be changed. We have a Zamboni that takes up so much time. It is so slow cleaning the floor. It does a great job, but why can we not speed it up? It takes two of them to clean an average space, but with a little speed, so much more could be done. Is speed really the answer for everything?

Speed in some cases should never be an option. Walking on the beach, holding hands, having dinner together, making love, kissing, laughing together, and hugging should all be taken slowly. These are just a few things that we have the mental capabilities of stopping time. When doing any one of these, they should never be rushed.

Take your time and soak up all the time together. Life is so short, and we have so many regrets later in life. For the few opportunities that we do have, we must seize that moment and leave nothing for regret. That means hugging a little longer, kiss a little slower, hold hands more firmly, laugh a lot more, eat together more frequently, and make love like it was your last night on earth. But whatever you do, do not rush anything with speed because once the time is gone, you'll never get time back.

4

POTHOLES

Potholes are a horrible thing to run over, and even worse when you don't see them until the last minute. By that time, you grind your teeth and hope it's not as deep as it appears to be. I have to wonder why someone travels the same road every day yet manages to run over the same pothole every time.

My only answer to that is, they become numb to the fact that they are doing it. It becomes second nature to them. Do they want to run over it? No. Chances are, they are not even aware of it until their car is riding funny and it needs very costly repairs. They sit and reflect while being reminded of the days driving over the same pothole and refusing to avoid it.

Relationships have potholes also. We get into a relationship, and we make a mistake, yet we fail to correct it on the spot. In some cases, it becomes weeks, months, and even years have passed. The problem has yet to be identified until one day your relationship takes a hard fall, and you cannot figure out what happened. Now you are forced to pay for help, miss work, and even spend time in court getting a divorce because the issue(s) were never addressed and remained in your daily life.

That is why I have cleared my schedule, and I have a date with my mind and soul to examine where I am in my life. No longer will I go with the assumption that I am doing everything correct. I must be honest with myself and make the changes that will help me be the best version of who you need.

I'm not doing this solely for us, but myself. I declare that I will no longer ignore my shortcomings and start to acknowledge the potholes in my life and the destruction they have caused. The last thing I desire to do is lose you because I failed to fill in my potholes.

5

NOTICE THE SMALL THINGS

The hardest part about having a vehicle is when you have to take it to the shop to get it looked at. No matter your status in life, we all hold our breath and hope that we do not get taken to the bank because more times than not, there is something wrong, and it needs a lot of work. Dealing with the engine is the worst that can happen. They always make you feel like you have to get the work done today, or the car won't be any good.

Well, have you ever sat back and thought about why the engine is not running well? Have you taken the time to recognize the small things that led to it? Are you keeping up with the oil changes and so forth? If not, that's the issue. It's not the big things that cause issues, but the smallest things that lead to being major problems.

That is why I want to notice and recognize all the small things within you. The way you walk when you're in relax mode. The way you walk when you're in a hurry. The way you talk softly on the phone or the way you look at me when you are in a good mood. I want to notice when you are in a bad mood, and you don't want to be bothered. I want to notice if you change shampoo or perfume. I want to notice how you stand when you are in the kitchen drinking water. I want to notice how you hold your phone while in a good gossip conversation. I just want to notice you.

I want to notice the way your smile looks when you laugh and the way your eyebrows look when you are in deep thought. I want to notice how you walk into the bedroom when you are in the mood for love, and I want to notice when you are not in the mood. I want to notice when you just need to be held or even kissed on the head.

I want to notice the way you put your favorite socks or pants on and stare in the mirror to remind yourself how beautiful and sexy you are. I want to notice you for the wonderful lady that you are. I vow to notice all the small things about you today, tomorrow, and forever because if I don't, somebody else will.

6

PURE HAPPINESS

When I first met you, I was in a sudden shock, and when we first exchanged emails, I was not sure what to say. I took a deep breath, collected my thoughts, and the first thing that came to mind is being respectful, nice, and trying not to sound so happy. But as I began to write, my fingers froze, and my mind went blank. No matter what I thought I wanted to say I could not. My impression of you immediately was in disbelief. Your beauty was something that I had never experienced. Writing a lady in your class was very unfamiliar to me.

So, I knew that if I was going to approach you through email that I had to have my words right. Not just any words but words from my heart and soul. It sounds kind of crazy considering it was my first email to you, but I already had so much respect for you without saying a word. You giving me a few minutes of your time was a dream come true. Once we started to chat back and forth, I realized that my first thoughts of you were wrong.

My thoughts of you after we started to talk were more than I could have ever imagined. You were perfect in my eyes. Your eyes, smile, hair, body, personality were beyond what I could have dreamed for, and I knew that my heart could love you. The day you walked into my life is a day that I will hold very dear to me.

People can take a lot of things from me, but they can never take the smile and the joy away from my heart that your smile brings to me. Thank you today, tomorrow, and forever for the happiness you have brought me. Kisses and enjoy your day.

7

NO MORE CAUTION

The traffic light, we all know it. We see it every day. Green is for go, yellow for caution, and red for stop. We all pretty much agree on the green and red, and no explanation is needed. But then there is the yellow light. It surely is a very tricky color because so many people see that light as being different. Depending on where you're from, that light is nothing but a different colored green or the color for stopping.

The fear of a ticket makes a lot of people stop and just catch the next green light no matter if you are in a hurry or not. The pain of proceeding is too much to deal with, so why bother. The color yellow also reminds me of the human heart and the emotions it is attached to. No one wants to be hurt, so they use caution when meeting someone new, and they do not put everything into it because of the fear of this being the wrong thing to do or being hurt.

I declare today that my caution light is gone, and I will give you and your heart everything I have. I am ready to take that major risk of the unknown because my heart tells me that I cannot go wrong with you.

Today I will deny any cautions that the world warns me about and just love you as I have never loved anyone before. I'm ready to step out there and accept anything that may be coming in my direction. I understand that this could be dangerous to my heart, but when I look at you, I have no fear, and I surely won't have any regrets tomorrow.

Today is the day that I take back the meaning of true love and believe that our lives, our paths have crossed for a specific reason. I have peace within myself from the decision that I have made. Your heart has shown me love, and today, no matter what, I will take my open heart and give you everything from my head to my feet. You have me completely, and I welcome you into my heart forever and ever.

As I finish this, I hold the tears back because this is what I dreamed love would feel like, and you are my dream life. You have given me the hope I have longed for, not to use caution and follow my inner soul to love like never before. Bye-bye hesitation and hello destiny. Kisses, and I am yours.

8

JUST ACKNOWLEDGE

As men, we differ so much from women. We think and act so much different. We tend to find it hard to talk about our emotions. God forbid our buddies think for one second that we are in touch with the emotional side of our human nature. As men, we tend to forget that we are who God made us, which was solely based on love.

We have to understand that even when we don't acknowledge who we are, it's still there. It's just like riding a bike. We can learn today, and not ride for years, but as soon as we get back on, we just take off. That is the same way that it should be when telling a lady how much you care about her. It is funny how a man will not express himself but will be ready to hurt someone else who tells their lady what they should be telling them. Why do we put ourselves through that?

So, I declare today that I will take that first step and declare my heart is open and full of love and passion for you. I am here to tell you, and anyone else in the world that will hear me, that I love you. I will proclaim from this day forth that you are that lady who lights up my day and makes me feel like any dream is possible.

You are my love, and I acknowledge that with every ounce of being in me. When I met you, I knew that it was time for a change. It was time to cry, a time of rejoicing, a time to let go and let love consume all of me. You have made me see that this world is nothing unless I can announce to all that you're the one. I feel as though I have crossed over in my life, and my life is filled with pure joy.

There is you and then everyone else. When you look in the mirror, I hope you see what I see and that one perfect lady that God did not just create, but he handcrafted you into this perfect lady who is the joy of each day and brightness in the dark. You are that lady who I adore today, tomorrow, and forever and ever. Kisses, and you are on my mind.

9

YOUR BEAUTY HAS SPOKEN

Beauty is in the eye of the beholder, but society has ruined that probably forever. It does not surprise me at all because it is all over TV. It is only getting worse, and the young generation is only getting more influenced.

TV, billboards, social media, newspapers, and everything in between has deemed that you have to look and be a certain way to find someone to want you. Image is everything in society, and love is based on it. Which is sad, but that is just the way it is.

Even I have found myself thing that way, so I am just as guilty. It is so bad that a person could lose all sense of reality when it comes to finding the right person. How many people have we let go because they did not meet the "status quo"? I must be honest, I truly did not know what I was getting into until that day you walked into my life, and at that moment, I knew exactly what it was.

Laying eyes on you for the first time was an eye-opener because, in my eyes, you are the perfect lady. I looked at your hair all the way down, and it was amazing. Did you meet what society deemed as the right shape, weight, color of skin, smile, or overall appearance? I do not know because I was blown away at you as a whole. You had yet to say a single word to me, but I felt it deep down in my soul and everything in me. You are it; you are the one that showed me what beauty in one person was supposed to look like.

We go a lifetime trying to feel that overwhelming excitement of finding that one person that "does it for you," and as a man, I finally reached mine. Looking upon you made me realize that beauty is not just in the eye, but it is in the very being of who we are. I now look upon your pictures for comfort, joy, motivation, visual enjoyment, inspiration, and it has become the best way to help my soul relax.

It is not just your beauty that I strive for, but it is you as a person and your beauty goes perfectly with your inner being to make what I call the perfect lady in many ways. You are my society's idea of beauty, and my drive to love and care for like never before. You are that lady who "does it for me." Thank you, and I seal this with a kiss on the nose.

10

BRINGING OUT THE BEST

When you are at your job, sometimes you work with a person that you see something good in them. They have this inside swagger. They are very cool, but as you get to know them, you start to see a major flaw in them. You see that they have zero ounces of confidence, and they have no idea what their true self-worth is.

You can see greatness in them, but they cannot seem to understand just how great they are at what they do. They need somebody who is willing to take the time to bring out the best in them. To motivate them to do better at what they are doing. Someone who inspires them like no other can.

That is what you are to me. You are my inspiration that I have searched for and longed for my whole life. You are that special lady that when I think of you, it seems as if the sky opens of possibilities that I did not think were possible before. Because of you, when I feel like giving up, I think of the love that you give me, and I get up and do great things. It is because of you that I can do what I enjoy, and that is writing. I have been looking for a reason, an inspiration, an outside drive that would help me pick up the pen and write again.

Just as I thought my life was going to go upside down, you walked into my life, and now my life is not only on the right track, but I seriously feel like I can achieve anything. I could never say thank you enough for being that one person that knows how to get me jump-started. When I think of you, I cry, not of sadness but joy, because the level of happiness that my heart has longed for has been located and captured.

You are the example of greatness in my world, and you are my world. With you, the world is perfect to me. With you, I see the glass as being full no matter how low it is because I have you, and with you, I have won the world around me. No more crying, no more long days, no more lonely nights because now I have you, and my world is just as I dreamed it would be one day. I miss you and have a great day.

11

ODD SUPPORT

The funny thing about support is that it comes in many different facets. Words, money, love, emotional or physical, but no matter which way it comes, it is very good and needed.

When people drive past a huge construction site or where major work on a building is being performed, where we often notice before anything else that someone is hanging off the side of it. We do not see the straps or anything, just someone hanging out there, and most take a deep breath, only to wonder how they can have the courage to do such a thing.

As we look closer, we can clearly start to see where their support is coming from and why they have such courage to do what so many people will not do. It is called the strap or safety line that keeps them in place and rooted where they are. Now, if that safety line breaks, then I guess we can consider things to go real bad real fast. It is only that one line that holds them, and they have to trust that it is going to hold and be there for them.

Today, you have my support, and I will be there for you. Whether you need a word of encouragement, a hug, or whatever I'm there for you. I want you to know that I truly believe in you, and I believe in all your dreams. My support to you is to help you reach your heart desires and to dream bigger every day. No dream or desire that you have is too little or too big, and you should reach for all of them starting today.

I believe in you with all my heart, and it's going to feel great to see you reach your dreams.

You are a very strong lady, and I see the fire in your eyes. You are ready to meet your dreams and exceed them. Use me in any way that you feel the need. When people look at you, I do not want them to see me, but only you. Leave them wondering, how does she get this roaring courage to get up every day to keep going and pressing for her heart desires? I am there for you today, tomorrow, and forevermore. Your dreams are waiting to happen!

12

I THINK I LIKE YOU

How do I say I like a lady like you? I am just a simple guy who does not have much. When I look at you, I smile. When I look at you, I feel sunshine over my life. When I think of you, I feel my soul drift into tranquility. When I see your eyes, I imagine the pure air on a bright early spring morning. When I envision your hands touching my hands, my entire body shivers with pleasure that all I can do is hold myself. I still feel your warm fingers all over me. Your eyes are my gateway to happiness.

Your lips remind me of a pink fluffy rose that has just blossomed. I want to hold your hips from behind and feel you lay your head back so I can feel your breath on my bare chest. I want to hold you as if my life depended on it. When I saw you, I knew that I wanted to lay you down on white sands and kiss you while I showed the world just how much I loved you. I would kiss you when the sun sets until it arises the next morning. I cannot stop thinking about you even for one second, and if I did, I feel like the beat of my heart would stop instantly.

I need your smile. I need your breath on my face. I need to be able to reach over in the middle of the night and kiss you on your stomach. My heart is with you every day, and I could not imagine a day without you in my life. I want your voice to be the first voice I hear every morning, and the last voice that I hear before I close my eyes at night.

My happiness came into existence the day that you came into my life, and I want to share my heart with you every day, all day. My heart has a genuine smile now because you are in my life. It is funny because I'm in training now, and my co-workers think I'm sitting here taking notes, but what I'm doing is writing you. The thought of you is what keeps me focused and helps me stay focused. The only reason that I write so much while I'm at work is that when I write you, I feel very close to you, and I feel at peace with life. Please never forget that I miss you so much.

13

ACQUIRED TASTE

Have you ever noticed some things are just not the same if you do not add seasonings, spices, sugar, salt, or whatever you desire to put in your food? You can try it with an open mind, but no matter what, it is always something missing. Is it a mental thing, or is it something else needed to make it taste better? Some people will say that it's all in your head, but when you know that something is not where it should be, you can never feel satisfied.

When this happens, you go out of your way to go through the cabinets, the pantry looking for that one thing that can make the food better to eat. Until you find it, you often consider not even eating it. Why? Because your desire to have that one thing that takes over you, and your taste buds want all or nothing.

At this point, you are craving this one thing so bad that you are willing to do anything to get your hands on it. For me, I love sugar in my grits. For some people, that is crazy to imagine. I will not eat them without sugar because they do not satisfy me. So, like all others, we are not eating anything that we do not like. A substitute will not do it. It is all or nothing.

This is the same concept when we find that one person that we know we really want to be with. We know that they are the seasonings, spices, sugar, salt, or whatever you desire. We must recognize that, and we have to treat them like they are the ones who complete us and makes our life better.

Often, too many times, we neglect that one thing that is the seasoning in our food when it's right there in our face. If it is there, why run to the cabinets or pantry looking for more or something else when all you need is sitting right there in your face.

Embrace it and treat that person like you need them to be that flavor that can quench that missing ingredient that would make your life all it was supposed to be. Do not be afraid to tell them that you need to shake up your life with them added to it. To give that kick and satisfaction that only they can do.

You would not wait more than a day to add salt to your food, so why would you wait another day to add that special person to your life. Let your voice be heard that your need them mixed into your life to be complete.

14

LET IT OUT

People always say never hold your anger or aggression inside because when you do that, it is never good when it comes out. I could not agree more. Look on TV and see how people's anger gets the best of them once they have had enough. They can do every imaginable thing under the sun; you name it, it can happen or has happened.

Anger coming out at the wrong time at the wrong place is not good for anyone involved. Now, wonder if a person has to keep love locked inside because they never had the opportunity to express that, and it was all bundled up. What would that be like when it came out. Well, I had no idea either until you came into my life.

The love that has been locked up and stored away for my whole life is ready to come out because you have given me the "green light" to love freely. I am ready to see what this is going to be like. I will write you all the time, I will tell you I love you in every other word, I will always open the doors for you when you're going and coming.

I would be waiting at the door to greet you with a hug and kiss. Dinner would be ready on the stove, and your favorite show recorded and ready to be watched. This is followed by a hot bubble bath with rose petals around the tub, soft music with candle aroma filling the room. There are so many things my heart is ready to do because of you. So many days of loving you are ahead of us. I have longed for this to come true for many years.

You have unlocked what I would describe as a heart bleeding of love that's ready to share everything and anything that you desire. I want to give you the love stored inside me that no one has allowed me to give, and I can't think or imagine any other lady that I would have wanted to unlock my heart.

You had my heart from hello, and now that you have it, I want you to know how thankful I am that you chose me. How will you use my heart today? It is completely up to you because I trust you more than anyone I have ever known. You are the one that has unlocked my heart, and now my love is ready to explode all over you.

15

I MUST WAKE UP

Waking up every morning is a new adventure for everyone, but most people have certain ways that they always prefer to start their day off. From drinking coffee, working out, praying, reading, writing, email, sex, or just whatever it may be. They cannot start their day until they complete their routine that helps them to focus and get the day started.

When they are not able to do the thing that helps them because they are running behind, they get up on the wrong side of the bed, and tend to have days that are long and frustrating. Now is that more of a mental thing or is it a valid excuse to have a bad day? Well, after a lot of thinking and mediation on what I feel would be a way that I would love to start my day, it's like this.

First and foremost, unless I'm waking up with you every morning, then this WILL NOT WORK FOR ME. I would not wake you up. I would first wake up and roll over and kiss you on the cheek and your neck. I would roll out of bed, walk to the other side of the bed, and kiss you on the head. I would walk out of the bathroom only to approach your side of the bed to kiss you again with a small bite on the cheek.

I would then proceed to get dressed but still keeping the noise down. I am in no rush, but I keep direct eye contact with you so I can take in all of your beauty. I would make my way back over to your side, get on both knees and lay my head on your hips while putting my arm around you. I would leave my head on your hips for about four minutes and enjoy the smoothness of your body. I would take in the aroma that comes off of your body.

I try to take in all of you so that I can have an everlasting smell with me of you all day. As I get up off my knees, I make my way up to your lips to finally get one good morning kiss. And just as I rise, I ask you to give me the tip of your tongue so I can have that.

I would lay my face on your face and whisper in your ear that I love you, and I hope you have an awesome day. As I walk away, I turn around, look at you, and say to myself, "That's the love of my life." You have made my morning the perfect morning.

16

BUILT-UP EMOTIONS

O n hot summer days when I was growing up, I'm reminded of how we would go in the back yard, turn the water hose on and get everyone wet. Oh, what a great time that was! We could not always afford to go to the public pool, so we had to settle for the next best thing, the water hose and sprinkling system to help cool us off on hot summer days.

The best part of it was bending the hose, while letting the extreme pressure build-up, is the exploding hose that let's out a massive amount of water at one time. The feeling of that water was great, and you could not wait for the next time to feel the same thing. It was a feeling that was everlasting.

It's the same thing for love in your heart. We tend to keep it all in because we have not been given that outlet to let it go and give it to that one special person. You have given a little away here and there but mostly kept it in for one reason or another. Well, you are that person I have decided to release my full love on.

You have unlocked my heart, and you showed me that it is ok to let my love explode all over your life. I am ready to let my guard down and allow the love that I have bundled up for so many years go wild and not hold back what I can offer in your life. Loving a lady like you has always been my dream, and now that you are in my life, my love has no boundaries. It's pure, and it is ready to be totally consumed by you.

Your smile and warm heart have shown me what real love is all about. You are the picture-perfect lady in my eyes, and I am happy that I have saved my heart for a lady just like you. Today I am officially ready to give my all and all. I seal this with a kiss on your nose.

17

REFLECTION TIME

As I arose this morning, I found myself sitting on the side of the bed reflecting. Not just reflecting on anything, but only one thing in particular. Something was pulling on my inner being immediately. I put my head down, and despite the room being filled with complete darkness, my eyes were closed as I was trying to grasp what was going on.

It was like I had an out-of-the-body experience, but it was such a relaxing feeling. I could not hear anything, but my sense of feeling was stronger than ever. I could not understand what was going on, but I loved the feeling that was going through me. I tried to get up, but something grabbed me and said, "Enjoy this surreal moment."

I was smiling so much, and a sense of happiness filled my body. I knew I was ready to take on the challenges of the day and overcome anything in front of me. I was still wondering what was causing me to feel this way, and all of a sudden, it hit. My experience this morning was because of you. I reflected immediately on you, and your smile and my smile suddenly went to pure excitement.

It was like I had a shot of energy and was able to forget about how much I wanted to go back to bed. Your smile was my motivation to get up and get going. You are so sweet and for you to be my friend is more than I could have ever imagined. People say that you must know someone for years to know them, but after meeting you, that idea was gone forever because I knew that you were special from the first hello. The first time I laid eyes on you, it was no doubt whatsoever that I knew you were special.

It was hard for me to imagine that a guy like me could ever talk to a lady like you. Now that we talk, I am still in disbelief because talking to you is a dream come true. So, allow me to say thank you for all. You are a wonderful lady, and I feel very honored that I'm your friend. This is a privilege, and I do not and will not ever take you for granted. Have a great day, and do not forget about me.

18

FOCUS ON WHAT'S IMPORTANT

It's amazing where we decide to put our priorities in life. For instance, we love sports, and it is a part of our everyday lives. We put so much effort and energy into our teams. From tailgates parties, buying gear online to make the games better. Months of pllanning for big games, writing it down all over, and talking to your friends about the upcoming day.

We get excited; lose our minds and everything in between. Granted, this is just a game, and believe me; I get hype about my teams also. And God forbid they lose. It is like your life is over, and you take it out on everyone around you. It is as if the world is coming to an end. But seriously, is this where our priorities should be so high?

I can think of better things to focus my energy on, something that at the end of the day matters the most. That is caring and loving for you. My focus is on you and making sure that your heart is happy while making sure that I do not forget to tell you that you make me the happiest man alive.

Assuring you every day that I cherish you and making sure that you know how honored I am that you are in my life. Without you, my life would be empty, and a huge void will be in my heart. From day one, you gave me a sense of love that has engulfed my heart and made me realize that you are the most important person in my life. That with you, the sun can shine, and with you, all my dreams can be achieved. You are an amazing lady, and I will always be excited about loving you.

I long for the day that you are in my arms. I will look you deep in those beautiful eyes with those perky cheeks, then giving you the longest and slowest kiss on the nose. Only to pause to smell your hair and run my fingers through it. I never want to let go because holding you is my way of holding on to the life that you have given me. For that I say thank you. I missed you yesterday, today, and forevermore. You are in my thoughts, and you have a great day.

19

DISCONNECTED

A couple of weeks ago I get in my car after driving it a few minutes prior and it will not start. The lights, radio, and what not was working but no power was coming from the engine. I was bummed out because just as I thought things were getting better for me, I run into this major issue with my car.

I had no idea what to do, and as much as I did not want to, I felt a small panic come over me. There was this disconnection between me and my car that I could not understand why. I examined everything I could, and no matter what, I could not find the source of the problem.

This reminds me of my life and how disconnected I was until the day that you walked into my life. You were just like my friend who came over and showed me exactly where the problem was, and after connecting a wire back, the car was perfect. And that is what you did when you walked into my life.

You connected to me to the one source that I was missing, and that was life and energy. You sparked my heart and gave me a new jump on life. You inspired me to smile even when there was nothing to smile about. I have a different get-up and go because my energy is driven by your love and how much you care for me.

If there was ever a time in my life that I needed someone, it is now, and you were there to catch me when I felt my life drifting away. Your heart is like a huge energy source that I have to tap into everyday. I realize that life is difficult, and things go bad, but with you as my connection to happiness, I know that my life is awesome. I can reach out to you and feel an immediate change in my heart.

I am addicted to you, and I can tell when I am running low. My goal is never to let you go and keep you in my heart so I can keep going. Thank you for connecting me to life. It is time to go tell the world have a life again, and it's because of you. Have a great day.

20

EYES OF BEAUTY

The amazing thing about life is the beauty that it holds. We all see beauty in many ways, and we tend to stir towards those things that our eyes find appealing. Sometimes finding that beauty that makes you smile from the inside out could take a while, but like most people, you will encounter it sooner than later.

I never understood or never really had a true appreciation for the meaning of art. I grew up where the arts and beauty were not an everyday language because it was about survival. So, it took me a while to understand what art was and the beauty that went with it. As I have gotten older and just a little more mature, I have realized each day what an art picture means to me.

When you look at something that appeases the eyes, it tends to stay with you. You become hooked on that beauty, and you long for it more. And just when you thought you had seen the most beautiful sites in the world, you realize in a matter of seconds that your eyes have not yet seen true beauty yet. Then the view of your face came into my eyes. At that exact moment, I truly understood what real beauty was.

It was you, and I knew that no matter what I looked at from here on would ever compare to you. Some days it's not fair because I base everything on your beauty and nothing seems to be worth my eyes to look upon. All I want to see is your face.

When I awake in the morning, the best way to start my day is to look at the real beauty that the day and my life have to offer. Your face represents what pure beauty is. It is a masterpiece of art. It has some of the qualities of something that should be kept under a lock and key to display to all those who appreciate the beautiful things that life has to offer.

Your beauty is my sunshine, and your beauty is what sends the blood through my veins at a rapid pace. Thank you for allowing me to look upon you each day and I send my thanks to you with a kiss. Have a great day.

21

IT WAS A LIE

When I was growing up and wanted to start dating, I was made to believe that when you meet someone that it was normal to take forever to get to know them. You never expressed your feelings out of the fear of so many things. I thought that it took years to know someone. Then I realized that you don't know anything more about a person after ten years than when you first met them.

You would act like you never had feelings, and if you kept your words and heart to yourself, then at the end of the day, you would be ok. Those were some hard habits to break, and you did not want to be the one who was caught being all sensitive and in touch with your emotional side per se.

Something changed in the blink of an eye for me. It was when I first saw you and found out that everything I had learned was a lie. Something instantly told me that you were so unbelievable and too good to be true. I knew when I saw you that day it was the day that I would tell you exactly how I felt.

I stood in the mirror and told myself that I would have to be stupid if I allowed myself to be deceived and not open up to you. You are a dream come true with a morning of fresh air. You make me have hope like never before. When I think of you, I try not to get emotional because I know you are a great lady with so much class. A lady for whom I have the highest level of respect!

When I met you, I immediately knew you would hold a dear place in my heart. I cannot express how happy you have made me in a very short period. I want the world to know from this day forth that you are the true diamond in my life. If I must broadcast that to the world, I can do that through your beautiful smile and your amazing heart.

You were yesterday, today, tomorrow, and forevermore the cornerstone of my heart. Have a wonderful day, and I miss you!

22

MYSTERY VISION

Last night I was tired, but as I was falling asleep, I had this vision. A vision that brought such peace over my body thatI could not figure out what it was or who it was. All I can remember is smiling as I dozed off, but something funny happened this morning. It was like that same image was awaiting me when I woke up.

I suddenly felt that same joy as I did last night. I still could not put my finger on it to clarify what it was. I was angry because I wanted to see what it is was that was causing all this joy over my body. As I got to the bathroom and switched on the light, the image was clearer than ever. It was so clear that I was so ashamed that I could not recognize it.

It was a ray of sunshine of your smile that was causing me so much joy. It was your hair that stood out that loomed, and I reached out to touch it, and it glided through my fingers. It was the smell of your neck that I tried to cover my body with. It was the shape of your perfect lips that I longed to connect my lips with.

Your hands felt like the finest silk that you get from the middle east that money can buy. Your face was the resemblance of the most beautiful sunset setting over a beautiful ocean and was the only source of light. Your whole being is radiant, and you are so perfectly made.

I closed my eyes because that is one vision that I want to hold on to for the rest of my life. I missed you yesterday, today, and forevermore. Please have a great day, and you are on my mind. I want relish in the moment because times like this are rare in a persons life.

23

I CAN GET THROUGH

Today is one of those days you wake up and realize just how priceless life is. You reflect on what and who is in your life. You find yourself smiling uncontrollably, and only you know why. It is because I can get up even before the sun rises and can write to say hello to such a special lady like you.

It is the moments like this that are never forgotten. It is times like this that I wish I could push pause on the world clock, to breath, cry, or to continue smiling because you never want to let go of moments like this. Because of you, I can do all of those things, and because of your smile and friendship, I know I can face all the challenges that I will face today. Nothing matters except right here right now.

It is only the vents from the air conditionor cutting off and the rest of the dead silence in the house and my deep thoughts of you. You are truly a lady worth thinking about and, without a doubt, worth daydreaming about. You are just that special. Thank you for your friendship yesterday, today, and forevermore.

You are my friend, and nothing else matters. I truly hope today for you is filled with smiles, laughter, hugs, and love. I am thinking of you now, and those thoughts of you will carry me through my day. Thank you, and have a great day.

24

I DREAMED OF YOU

When I was a young boy/young man, I would always sit and daydream about what I wanted out of a lady. I guess you can say, my dream girl. The type of style she would have, how she carried herself, her hair, and her natural scent from her shin. I wondered how her smile would look and if it would light up the when she entered a room filled with people. Who would she inspire by her presence and motivate when she was around?

I wondered if she would be a lady of dignity and respect for herself and others. I wanted a lady who I could wake up in the middle of the night and stare at and wondered how I could be so lucky to be lying next to her. A lady who would let me freely express myself and allowed me to be me. A lady who would lean on me and allow me to lean on her.

A lady when times get hard, stands firm and fights with me. That is a great lady to envision having in my life. And then one day I saw you and right before my eyes my dream became a reality. You were everything that my vision was and then some.

Some people say dreams do not come true, but meeting you was out of this world. I do not know what today or tomorrow holds, but all I know is the excitement that you bring to my life today. You are the purest example of God's perfect work, and when I look at you, it's like looking at a miracle. You are an exceptional lady and having you on the other end is an exceptional way to live life. You are above all and you are the lady of my dream.

25

COMPROMISE

Imagine a newlywed couple buying their first house together. The wife wants that elegant kitchen that her friends will love. The beautiful bathroom that she can soak in her hot water. The husband just wants a nice garage where he can fix it up and make it his go-to place. Or even a place in the house that he can create as the man cave that all men want.

The man does not have much that he really wants and is willing to compromise what he desires so she can be happy. We see compromising in so many different areas of life. We compromise on what car to drive, the school to attend, or even just going out with the family to eat. No matter what, someone will feel that they did not get what they desired.

In a relationship, both people need to understand when to compromise on something. Are there things that do not need to be compromised on? With me, the basic things that should never be compromised you get. Love, respect, compassion, honor, and loyalty should come with any relationship.

If you are with me, you can be rest assured that everyday that I am granted life, you will receive the basic parts of a relationship that should never be taken for granted and or compromised. Being with me is a guaranteed kiss everyday, night, and day. A love you have spoken about countless times. A man that will not only listen to what you are saying but who actually hears what you are saying from the heart.

Everyday might not be perfect, but you will get my smile and support. If you cannot get those basic things from me, then I am no good to you, and that is why I strive to have a no-compromise of the basic needs policy. Some things can be overlooked, but seeing you smile will never be one of them.

26

THROUGH CONCRETE

Have you ever taken a walk and just noticed how grass grows in the middle of the road or on the sidewalks? It puzzles me every time I see that. I ask myself, how can something so hard and solid have something so delicate like grass growing up through it. It is one of those great mysteries that we can never seem to figure out.

Even when you cut or pull them out, they always seem to come back. It is like they are just destined to be in that location. They cannot be discouraged or moved away from the spot they are growing in because they know exactly where they belong. What if we were that way when we are in relationships? What if we get in a relationship and remain that way?

How does a relationship look if we dedicate ourselves when we are with someone? We have so many outside distractions that can possibly uproot our relationship. We have gossip, social media, friends, and sadly family. These are the strong forces that so many people cave into when those distractions arise.

We allow those issues to come in and uproot the one relationship that we have dreamed about our whole life. We need to be like the grass and know exactly where we belong. The wind will blow, storms will come, blizzards will freeze things out, but you need to know that this is where you should be.

We must understand that being in a relationship, things will never be the same everyday. When the relationship can bloom like grass coming through the concrete with all beautiful leaves, so can a relationship. Two people must understand that they have to be rooted. No matter what, outside forces try to destroy it, they stay committed.

27

GREAT TEAMMATES

In 2015, the Kentucky Wildcats basketball team experience one of the best college basketball seasons of any team in history. They tore through college teams like it was the easiest thing in the world to do. Blowing out teams by 30 or so points every night was the common thing to do. They loved playing together, and you should see that through their body language.

How did they get to that point? Most of them were freshmen, and sophomores, with only a few days together on campus. They were able to go to classes together, a trip to the Bahamas, bowling together, videos and dinner together. This sounds like the making of a great relationship in the making. All the ingredients to a great recipe were there to be mixed. They bonded on purpose, and the results were incredible.

That is exactly what a relationship is all about, teamwork. The building of their bond and pursuing to be great teammates was the overall mission of the relationship. The building of a great relationship goes through the process as the Kentucky team did to build that tight-knit bond. The relationship does through many different adventures while looking to get to know each other.

Two people take trips, and they go to dinner, some play video games, bowling, fishing, and on-and-on. No two relationships do it the same, but the end results should all be the same. They can count on each other just like good teammates depend on each other. No one person is above the other. They had strong communication skills, they supported each other, and they cared for them, which builds strong relationships.

If you're going to be in a relationship with anyone, make sure you can call them your teammate because the victory of being together is, is like winning a champonship.

28

YOUR CHOSEN PLACE

We have so many places that we can say is our favorite place to relax. One place that people drive hours away to relax is the beach. They can sit and stare at the ocean for hours at a time. The seagulls, the wind blowing, and the sounds of the waves crashing in. They arrive in a place mentally where nothing matters. We watch the waves come and go only to sink deeper into a place of pure tranquility.

Bills, problems of life, nor work matters, and it's almost like we forget that we have anything bothering us. People plan their whole vacation time around just being at the beach and sitting next to the water. To only stare out as far as the naked eye can see. Getting the well-needed rest they have been daydreaming about for so long. When they get there, it has been all worth the wait of the big climax arrival.

So why can't we arrive at our homes with this kind of excitement? Why can't we be sitting at work with the thought of going home each day be just as exciting as going to the beach? Why can't we get in our cars and smile all the way home? Why does going home have to be such a dreadful time for so many people?

No one should have to go home to a spouse or lover with a dreadful face. Why one should want to stay at work just because going home is a hard time for them. Why should anyone just hate going? Why should it be war at home, the place that is supposed to bring you joy and relaxation? So many people face these real-life feelings every day.

When you are in a relationship, going home each day should be an exciting time. You should be so happy to get home that time seems to stop that last hour of the day at work. Being at home should be that peaceful time that we are all can embrace.

It does no good to be in a relationship if going home each day is the worst part of the day. The home is where we all should find refuge and peace. We find kindness and love. Homes are where we go after a long day to be around the ones we love the most. If being in a relationship is all about being with that person that you love and care for, then going home to that person would be that must more important.

It's so important that we find that love to go home to daily. When you find that happiness, that is equal to taking a vacation. You go home, and you separate yourself from the outside and lock yourself in with the person who adores, loves you, cares for you, and cuddles with you. When you are with the right person, your home will be your beach, with nothing but relaxing sounds and memories that will last a lifetime. Make home your real refuge.

29

TODAY

Today is one of those days that is not like yesterday, and not sure about tomorrow. But right here, right now, I smile because you are in my life. I delight in your smile and shiver at your heart. You are amazing, and I am happy that today you're in my life.

No one knows tomorrow's fate, so today, while there is breath in my body and my mind is sane, I tell you that I cherish you. I am very honored that I can pick up my phone and have direct communication with you. I hold you and your heart very close to mine. My happiness today is because of your love. You are such of a lady that I put so above life itself.

Thank you for everything, and you will always be in my heart. Regardless if we talk every day, once a week, or once a month, your place is rooted in my heart. Thank you so much. Kisses and have an amazing day. No matter what you are doing or where you're at, you're in my heart and thoughts.

30

JUST MIX IT

Cooking shows have become so popular over the years. During the lockdown of many restraunts, people were forced to cook more than in the recent past. They would watch as many cooking shows as possible. They enjoyed watching the chefs show all of their ingredients. Some people were not familiar with some of the ingredients, while some regularly use those ingredients.

In the beginning, the way the ingredients were are all mixed together may look very un-tasteful. Most people would never even consider mixing certain things together. The chef knows exactly the outcome he is going for. The viewer might not have the same vision for the outcome, but the chef stays focused on what he knows can be something very special. The outcome is exactly as he planned it to be. Others cannot see it and are in shock. After all, they could not see the end because they were too worried about the beginning.

Relationships are the exact same way. Two people get together and they are almost completely different. They do not talk the same, act the same or even like the same things in some cases. They also cannot see themselves together because it is not a good mix. They try to interact just to see what happens. They start spending more and more time together, only to see they are better together than they could have imagined.

The outside view of family or friends starts to way in and give their views because they only see two people who are not in their eyes a good match. They try to do everything they can to see them not be together and break them up. With their naked eye, they just can't imagine these two people together. They find it gross and often say I would never date him or her because of their outer appearance.

The two people shutout all the chatter of the naysayers, focus on each other. They realized that they are good people, but together they have greatness inside. They are a strong team that has bonded that only they can see. They tune out any negative talk, and they focus on what they have made since mixing up their lives together.

Most people could not see what they could become because they were too focused on how they looked like as a couple in the beginning. They were not behind doors with the couple, so they could not see how the ingredients were all coming together. When all is said, the ingredients have bonded perfectly. With the right heat and pressure, anything can be created. Now the world can fully understand how two mixed-up people could turn out to be something so special.

31

OH!! YOU MESSY

One thing I have learned over the years is the magnitude of having a clean desk. Before I was forced to keep my desk clean, I thought I had everything under control. Everything was in its proper place, and I knew exactly where things were. I had my system down, and I was able to work despite having things all over the desk.

People would come to my desk, and they would just stare out of disbelief at how messy I seemed to be. People tried to ask me why my desk looked so bad. They even gave me a look like they did not trust that I knew my job, simply because my desk was so out of the norms. They would even go out of their way to avoid talking to me about work, it was so bad.

Then one day, that all changed. I got a new boss, and he was not having that. You could see his face change colors when he saw just how much clutter I had on my desk. He sat me and explained that by the end of the day, my desk would be spotless, or he was going to counsel me. I did understand why he was so upset, but soon my understanding would be clear.

The whole time I thought I had a great system. After all, it was my clutter that I had created. I always stressed out because I thought I had more word to do than I actually had. No matter how much I thought knew where everything was, I realized how much extra pressure I was putting on myself. The fear of never getting things done because of the clutter distracted me from what was important.

We do our relationships the same way. We allow so much extra clutter into our relationships that do not need to be there. It is so bad that we lose focus on the one person that we stop seeing as the most important person in our lives. Even when we see the warning signs, we still allow things that don't belong to hang around.

These bad things can be habits, actions, or things that, at the end of the day, really do not matter in the big scheme of things. We allow things and people to be in our lives that should never be there, but our eyes are blinded by the mess we allow to arise in our lives.

We have to arrive at the point where we can see clutter from a mile away and do whatever it takes to keep our desks clean so we can continue to see the important things in our lives. When you clean off your desk, the pressure of things will soon leave, and you will see that you have more time to do things with that special love one.

So, never look at decluttering your life as a task or a burden but view it as a chance to see the beauty that you once before adore looking at. The system that you thought you had will be nothing but a memory because the new outlook will be one that you will cherish forever.

32

THE RIGHT KEY

If you are like most people around the world, there is one consensus person we all love and hate all at the same time. A locksmith is a close number one in all of our books. We love it when a locksmith shows up because we have locked our self out, and getting back to our normal life is only a few minutes away. We hear that click, and things are all good again.

When we hear that click, we also know it's time to pay up. Let us be real, three to five minutes of work for almost $65-100. We suddenly go from smiling to a bit of anger and disbelief that we must pay that for such fast work. After that, we have a self-anger within ourselves for allowing ourselves to be so careless as to lock ourselves out. We vow that from now we will be careful and never allow that to happen again.

So, why do we do that in our own relationship? Why do we have a person in our life that has opened the lock to our heart, yet we choose to lock them out when they are finally able to get inside? How can we be so careless as not to recognize when we are about to lock out the one person that was meant to unlock our heart. Why are we shutting them out.

The person has paid the fee to unlock it, but we still find ways to kick them out without any form of repayment. Some people invest so much time to prove their love to another person, only to be left hanging because we assume that it will be someone else who unlocks their heart.

We run that person away, only to have nothing but regrets later in life. We knew that the person unlocked our heart at the right time, but we still find a way to mess that up in one way or another. We always think that if someone can unlock our heart it can be in a much deeper way. In reality, the person, who is in your life, is the one who is meant to be there.

Embrace the person with the right key that has unlocked the right door. When you look past them, you could be looking past a lot more than you could ever imagine. Follow your heart and let it guide the key straight in so your happiness and joy can always be unlocked. Sometimes when something is locked, there is no key ever to fit it again. Don't be the one with the permanently locked heart because you're too selfish to see what is clearly in front of you.

33

DON'T TAINT THE VISION

The military has many different accessories at their disposure. From weapons, ships, plans, equipment, and so much firepower that overtakes the enemy in no time. The one thing that seems to be overlooked the most is the use of night vision goggles. Many missions are performed at night, in areas so dark that you cannot even see your hands in front of your face.

When they put on the night vision goggles, the whole game changes. Things become a lot easier to see than before. Now, they can see things that the naked eye could never see under those circumstances. With those goggles, the whole scene can be viewed.

People who think they can hide, can be identified almost instantlty. No movement goes unnoticed, and the ability to see what no one else can is possible. A great tool to have that not all have the ability to have access to.

We have that same vision ability in our love life. We are with someone, but we fail to acknowledge what we see right in front of our faces. We know we have power with our words, yet we fail to open up and say what we feel.

The date or marry a person, who we know is very special. We see things that no one else seems to see, but we fail once again to speak up. We think that we can limit our communication because of the mindset of there is always tomorrow to say what we see and feel.

The truth is we do not have until tomorrow. Someone is always waiting in the wind to say what you failed to say. They are ready to voice what they also see that is well overdue. So, my advice to say something while you have the chance. Stop assuming they know what you are thinking. Never take them for granted.

You're only one day away from losing what your eyes and heart have been showing you from day one; they are special and a great person. Open-up today because once they walk out the door, your vision of them no longer matters!

34

DON'T GET BLOWN AWAY

I love the weather when there is a nice steady breeze. You can sit back and enjoy it for hours on end. The flowers are waving back and forth in the wind. This has to be a great day for all who can witness it. In the midst of this, other things are also blowing, more specifically paper.

Unlike flowers, the paper is not grounded to anything. The wind picks up the paper, tosses it. It goes up and down just as the wind pleases. The paper is lifeless, with no control over anything, it is literally under the mercy of the wind. It can blow go as high or as long the wind has the power to do so.

As humans in a relationship, should have complete control over what we do. The rumors will blow high, and they will come from every direction. People outside the relationship will have so much to say because, quite frankly, they do not want to see others happy.

We cannot let the strong winds of others voices blow us out of a great relationship. Do not get caught up being sucked into those who have nothing else better to say or do. You know in your heart that you

67

have a great relationship, and now is the time to be tree-rooted. Don't be that piece of paper that gets tossed around with minimum pressure. Your relationship is strong, so stay rooted.

35

REACH THE TOP

Exercising is not any fun at all. Most people choose not to do it because it hurts so bad. The key is to find what you enjoy doing that will help to maximize the impact on reaching your goals. For me, it's the stair master or finding as many steps as possible. I know how hard it is, and honestly, I hate it, but the impact is fast and enormous.

Today while working out with 11 floors of steps, it hit me while I was bent over grabbing my knees. It was all clear to me when I felt like giving up that each level represented my bad eating habits. Things that I knew would destroy me and stop me from being a healthy person. The levels represented things such as ice cream, fast food, chips, soda, bacon, grits, and on-and-on.

I realized that getting to the top of each level, despite how hard it would be, was a symbol of destroying my bad habits. The 11th floor represented a longer and healthier life. No matter how hard it got, no matter how many times I asked myself, why am I even trying to change. I knew people were counting on me to be around longer, so destroying those habits was very crucial. The top was right there, waiting for me to decide what's more important, my habits or those I loved the most.

Relationships are not any different than working out. We get in a relationship, but we still manage to form toxic habits that, in the end, will destroy us. We see the signs, we know the sign, but we refuse to use our better judgments. We think we are strong, and we play around with things that were never meant for us to engage with. It's all meant to take us away from the one person who we adore and love the most.

Even after seeing how hazardous the habits are, we have become so addicted that it's a normal part of our life. Does not mean it's good, but we are hooked to doing it. Everyone has their own thing that they know it's time to let go of, but we choose not to, putting at risk everything we hold with value.

Like that ice cream, it so hard to stop eating. We must recognize who and what is on the 11th waiting for you. We must attack ever how many levels it requires to get to the goal of making sure your relationship is not ruined because you choose your bad habits over what's most important.

If you know you have someone up there at the top waiting on you, then you must do everything humanly possible to break those habits. The rewards have to outweigh the habits. You must recognize how critical it is to make changes because once that person gets tired of waiting at the top for you to show up, they are gone. You have spoken to what's most important to you. So, the same way that you attack your worst exercise to be healthier, you have to attack your habits for the sake of your relationship.

36

SET IT AND GO

While in the military, I never really used an alarm clock. People around me did, and they all seemed to live by it. It was not until after I retired, not working for a long period of time that I started to use the alarm clock to get up for appointments.

I had just moved into a home, and I realized how satisfied it felt to sleep all night.

I did not have to get up multiple times a night to check to see what time it was. It was just set it and sleep all night. My body felt so refreshed each morning. I felt mentally and physically better. I asked myself why for so many years, I never used one of these great things.

So much energy and sleep were lost because I had gotten so accustomed to this way that I had no idea what I was missing out on. All I had to do was set and go; instead, I ignored the better choice.

We have to approach our relationships the same way. We have to get used to doing things the right way. It has to be automatic, without a second thought. Once that alarm was set, I did not have to check it every day to make sure that it was going to go off.

We have to be so deliberate about our actions. Anything that changed in the smallest way would be noticed. Our actions of love and caring should be the norm. Our loved ones should never have to wonder if you really care about them or not.

Your actions should be automatic. You just do it like you don't even think about it. Not saying you always have to be predictable, but certain things will always just be there. So figure out what should be automatic in your relationship, then set it and go.

37

THE RIGHT COLOR

In a years' time women have so many days that are for them. Without naming all, you have Valentine's Day, anniversaries, birthdays and Mother's Day. Clearly these are days that women look forward to more then men. Now, for men we have that one time of the year that we love. The days we can get outside on the grill with our family and friends. It is the day we can call ourselves the man of the house.

The grill is the place we love to be at. Wait, before you say women can get on the grill also, you are correct. But for goodness sake give us that one moment. We like to talk smack, drink and just have a good time. The only thing that so many men disagree on is how they like to cook their meat and how they prefer the inside of a juicy thick steak to look.

Some prefer blood running out, slightly pink or well done. This will always be an argument, but when a man knows what he likes he sticks to it because it fits what he thinks is a great steak. You can give your thoughts on why you prefer it a different way, but he will not budge because he knows exactly what he likes.

Relationships need to get to the same point as discussion as the color of the steak. Each has to find a system that works for them. There are so many different versions of what a relationship looks like on the inside, but each couple has to find the color that works for them and stick to it.

Yes, you can see how others do their relationship, and it might be working great, but that does not mean it will be the exact color of what you need for your relationship. No two colors will be the same. It's very important that you narrow down what works and not be wavered by what others are doing. Find the right temperature that cooks your relationship to that color that is only meant for you and your love.

38

WONDER

I wonder how you are doing. I wonder if you are smiling or if you're even in a good mood. I wonder if having me in your life is as wonderful as it is having you in my life. I wonder if you ever miss me so much that life around you sometimes stops existing. I wonder if my emails or my words touch your soul like they do as I write them. I wonder if my emails do anything to put a smile on your face when you read them, or they are so kind and sweet that you must read them over and over sometimes. I wonder if you read them or just delete them and hold the words that I wrote deep in your heart.

I wonder if you long for the touch of my hands when we cannot be together or if you call me just to hear my voice to make everything seem alright. I wonder if being Mrs. Spencer is something that you enjoy more than anything in this world. I wonder if when I hold you in my arms you get chills on your body and long for the day that I never have to let go of you. I wonder if I get on your nerves to the point where you do not even want to be around me or talk with me. I wonder what I can do to always keep you smiling and in love with me.

I wonder what kind of destruction path I would be on if I never met you, and I wonder why It took me so long to cross paths with you in this world. I wonder when you say my name to your self do you feel great love and feel the sense that everything is going to be ok. I wonder why our phone conversations are never like the talks we have in person. I wonder when we get off the phone, was I bore to you, or I wonder do I call or email too much. But overall, I mostly wonder will we stay in love until the end of time.

What I do not wonder about is how much I need you in my life. I never wonder how easy it to love a lady that is special as you. I never wonder if marrying you was the best thing I have ever done. I never wonder if starting a family with you would be a problem, but on a blessing from God. I never wonder about what it takes to love you the way that you need to be loved. I never wonder if I should skip a day from telling you that I love you so much. I never wonder if I could give you the world or not would I because I would in a second.

I never wonder how it's going to feel to buy our 1st home together. I never wonder if it will feel good or not to wake up with you for the rest of my life. I never wonder if fighting for our relationship was not worth it because it is worth more than you know. I never wonder if giving you a kiss before I leave for work every day is an option or laying my face in your chest to listen to your heartbeat. Mostly I will never wonder if spending the rest of my life with you was the wrong decision. Please never wonder if I love you or not, because I do and always will.

Made in the USA
Columbia, SC
13 February 2023

11869708R00046